I need
a hug.
Will you Cuddle
me, Lou?

What?
With those
spikes?
Get
away from
me!
Shoo!

I need a hug. Will you cuddle me, Ken?

Help! It's that prickly thing at it again!

I need a hug. Will you cuddle me, Moe?

Cuddle you?
NO, I won't!
No No
NO NO!

No-one will
hug me.
That's
not very kind.

But, *hey!*
Wait a
minute . . .

YOU'VE ALL

CHANGED

YOUR MIND!

Geez,
all I did was ask
for a *kiss*.

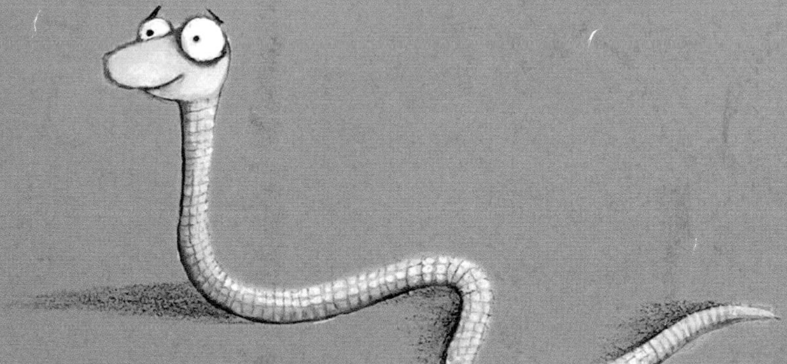

Well, isn't this lovely?
Yes, how about this.